The Emperor's New Clothes

The Emperor's New Clothes

RETOLD AND ILLUSTRATED BY

Suçie Stevenson

Adapted from a story by Hans Christian Andersen

A Yearling First Choice Chapter Book

E blu   E - Blu
A,J

Published by
Bantam Doubleday Dell Publishing Group, Inc.
1540 Broadway
New York, New York 10036

Library of Congress Cataloging-in-Publication Data
Stevenson, Suçie.
The emperor's new clothes / retold and illustrated by Suçie Stevenson.
p.   cm.
"A Yearling first choice chapter book."
Summary: Two rascals sell a vain emperor an invisible suit of clothes. In this
version of the fairy tale, the characters are all animals.
ISBN 0-385-32246-1. — ISBN 0-440-41241-2 (pbk. : alk. paper)
[1. Domestic animals—Fiction. 2. Fairy tales.]
I. Andersen, H. C. (Hans Christian), 1805–1875. Kejserens nye klæder. II.
Title.
PZ10.S618Em 1998
[E]—dc20   96-2220 CIP AC

I Stevenson,
Suçie
✓ Title.
(Hans Christian)
m.e. Andersen, H. C.
1875

The text of this book is set in 17-point Baskerville.
Book design by Trish Parcell Watts
Manufactured in the United States of America
March 1998
10 9 8 7 6 5 4 3 2 1

Contents

1

Clothes Crazy

"I love clothes!" cried the Emperor.
"I don't care about anything else.
I don't have to! I'm the Emperor!"

"He's so spoiled,"
said everyone at court.
"Bring me my new hat.
No! No! You TWIT!"
snapped the Emperor.
"My other new hat!"

"B-B-But Your Majesty
has two dozen
brand-new hats!"
said the Emperor's First Valet.
"Fool!" said the Emperor.
"You're finished!"
He clapped his hands.
"Bring me a new First Valet!"

The Emperor always wanted
something new.

A Baron brought him
delicate cloth that glittered.
"Oooh, sparkly!" cooed the Emperor.

A Duke delivered bolts
of bright silks and satins.
"Oooh, slippery!" giggled the Emperor.

A Duchess gave him velvet
as soft as puppy fur.
"Oooh, cuddly!" sighed the Emperor.
The Emperor snapped his fingers.
"Now bring me something
really fabulous!"

11

2

Magic Cloth

One day two Swindlers came to town.

"They say the Emperor
is greedy and stuck up.
He sounds like an easy guy to fool,"
said Jack. "And he has tons of gold!"
"Let's trick him!" said Peter.

The two Swindlers told lies

to everyone they met.

"I'm famous!" said Jack.

"I'm even more famous!" said Peter.

"We are the finest weavers

in the world! No fooling!"

14

"Soon the Emperor will be
begging us to make him
a fancy suit!" said Jack.
And so the Emperor did.

The Emperor gave the two Swindlers
a room in the palace.

"Find the biggest loom in the empire
and set it up!" said the Emperor.

"Just wait, Your Highness," said Jack.

16

"We are going to weave something
that nobody has ever seen before!"
"You won't believe your eyes!"
said Peter.
"Yes! Yes!" cried the Emperor.

"It's going to be magic cloth!" said Jack.
"Only the very smartest people
will see it. People unfit for their jobs
won't be able to see it either."
"Oh, goody!" thought the Emperor.
"I can test all my friends!
What fun!"
Out loud, he said, "Excellent!

If you need anything, just ask!"

"Now that you mention it,"

said Jack, "a couple of bags of gold

would help get things started."

3

More Gold!

The two Swindlers asked
for thread made of gold and silver.
They asked for thread of every
color in the rainbow.
"Bring them a cartload!"
said the Emperor.

The two Swindlers hid
everything away to sell later.
"This is too easy!" said Peter.
"Hey, it's not easy to lift
all my bags of gold!"
said Jack. "Gold is heavy!"

The Emperor got curious.
"Lord Stinklestreet,
go see what my weavers
are up to!" he said.
"Lord Stinklestreet thinks
he's such a smarty-pants,"
giggled the Emperor.
"We'll see!"
Lord Stinklestreet opened the door
of the weaving room.
The two Swindlers sat
in front of an empty loom.
Lord Stinklestreet rubbed his eyes.
"I can't see the cloth!
This can't happen to me!"
he thought.

"Don't you love the
peacock pattern on the edges?"
asked Peter.
"P-P-Peacocks?" said the Lord.
"Why . . . yes! . . . Splendid!
Keep up the good work!"
said Lord Stinklestreet.
Lord Stinklestreet raced
back to the Emperor.

"Magnificent!
Green-and-blue peacocks!"
he spluttered.
"You are going to love it!"
"Excellent," said the Emperor.
"Send the weavers more gold!"

Lord Pumpernickel

The Emperor was curious as a cat.

"Let's see. Who shall I send next?

You! Lord Pumpernickel!"

called the Emperor.

"Check on the weavers.

Report back!"

Lord Pumpernickel watched
the weavers carefully.
As hard as he tried,
he could see nothing!
"Jack! Pass me that scarlet
thread!" said Peter.
"You've got it, buddy!" said Jack.

Lord Pumpernickel shook his head.
"I'm an idiot!" he thought.

"I wove in the sun and the stars—
that was my idea!" said Peter.
"Isn't it amazing how pure gold
thread glitters?"
"Ummm . . . Well, yes! YES!"
said Lord Pumpernickel.
"I can hardly stand it!"

Lord Pumpernickel
knelt before the Emperor.
"Thrilling, Sire!
They have woven the sun
and all the stars
into a brilliant cloth!"
"Nice going, Pumpernickel,"
said the Emperor.
"Send more gold to the weavers!"

The Emperor made half his court
go to look at the magic cloth.
"Great colors!" they said.
"Wondrous patterns!"
"Scrumptious texture!"
"They've even begun sewing!"
"People are smarter than I thought!"
grumbled the Emperor.

What a Suit!

Candles burned all night
in the windows
of the Swindlers' room.
"See how hard they work!
That's why they are the best!"
said the Servants.
If anyone was looking,
Peter snipped at the air
with his scissors.

Jack sewed tiny stitches
with an empty needle.
"Done!" cried the two Swindlers.
"Tell the Emperor his
fabulous suit is ready!"

The Emperor arrived for his fitting.
Peter and Jack pretended
to hold up the new clothes.
"What do you think?"
the two Swindlers asked.

The Emperor stood speechless.

"I see nothing!" he thought.

"Everyone else is smarter than me!"

"AHErr . . ." The Emperor

cleared his throat.

"What an extraordinary suit!"

he choked out.

The Emperor took off his clothes.

"Slip into this, Your Majesty!"

said Peter.

He held out a pair

of invisible trousers.

"OOOoooh! Lovely!"

said the Courtiers.

The Emperor preened

in front of the mirror.

"Try this, Your Excellency!" said Jack.

Jack pretended to give him a tailcoat.

"AAAAAAHhhhh! Handsome!"

said the Courtiers.

The Emperor did a little spin.

"Pardon me, I think this sleeve
is a little long," said Jack.
"You think?" said Peter.
"Any fool can see that!"
said the Emperor. "Fix it!"

38

"Is my new suit absolutely perfect
now?" asked the Emperor.

"You bet!" said Peter.

"Perfectamento!" said Jack.

The Emperor smiled.

"Give the weavers a lot more gold!"
he shouted.

6

Tee Hee

"Get ready!" called the Emperor.

"Get my fancy canopy!

Get lots of servants!

I feel like a parade!"

The Emperor marched proudly

through the city.

40

Everyone wanted to see
the famous suit.
No one wanted to seem stupid.
So the Grocer cheered,
"Simply breathtaking!"
"Unbelievable!" called the Baker.
He started the crowd
clapping and whistling.

"What a spectacular suit!"
yelled a Tailor.
A little girl pulled
on her mother's hem.
"Up! Hold me up!
I want to look!" she said.

"Momma!" cried the little girl.

"The Emperor has no clothes on!"

"Shhh! Shhh!" said the Mother.

"You know," whispered the Mother,

"she's right!"

"So she is!" said the Father. "Hah!"

The crowd started to rustle and hum

as people passed the word.

Someone shouted,

"The Emperor is naked!"

"He's totally starkers!" yelled another.

"Not a stitch on!" squealed a third.

The Emperor blushed bright red.

"I am a complete ninny!" he thought.

He lifted his chin.

He straightened his crown.

And he kept walking, faster and faster.

"Tee hee teee heee.

TEEHEEEHHHEEE HAH HA HAH!"

roared the crowd.

"HAR! HAR!" laughed Peter and Jack.

"Fooled you!" they shouted.

And they galloped away,

faster and faster,

with all the Emperor's gold.